MW01255184

Mojdeh Baratloo / Clifton J. Balch

ANGST:
Cartography

with "Cities & Desire 5" from *Invisible Cities* by Italo Calvino

SITES/Lumen Books
446 West 20 Street
New York, NY 10011

©1989 Lumen, Inc.
Printed in the United States of America
ISBN 0-930829-10-7

This publication replaces a regular issue of SITES Magazine.

Special thanks to the Sanborn Map Company of Pelham, New York, for permission to reproduce their maps.

"Cities & Desire 5" from *Invisible Cities* by Italo Calvino, ©1972 by Giulio Einaudi editore s.p.a.; translated from the Italian by William Weaver, ©1974 by Harcourt Brace Jovanovich, Inc. Reprinted by permission of the publisher.

SITES/Lumen Books are produced by Lumen, Inc., a tax-exempt, non-profit organization. Lumen, Inc. is supported, in part, with public funds from the New York State Council on the Arts; The New York City Department of Cultural Affairs; The National Endowment for the Arts; as well as with private contributions.

If our thinking manifested itself in the shape of a city, then we should of necessity come to the labyrinth.

Nietzsche

CONTENTS

As postulate, *ANGST: Cartography* re-envisions a neglected section of New York City's industrial infrastructure by extracting drawn images from an existing cartographic system (Sanborn Maps) and the cityscape. The resulting drawing/maps, partially based on existing physical elements and partially derived from metaphor, respond to a sector of New York in abstract cartographic form—one that could stimulate new perspectives for directing a late 19th- and early 20th- century semi-industrial wasteland toward the

21st century.

The project is the result of architects Moji Baratloo and Clif Balch's line and plane dialogue with the Gowanus Canal area of Brooklyn, initially executed for a 1982 group exhibition, *The Monument Redefined*, and expanded in 1988 for an installation at The Institute for Contemporary Art, P.S. 1 Museum. Their design, a series of manipulated cartographic images, was reinforced by literary underpinnings when Baratloo and Balch found the project evolving as a response to a physical place, as well as to Italo Calvino's "Cities & Desire 5," from *Invisible Cities*. They appropriate Calvino's story of silence, memory, and the founding of the city of Zobeide as a running text, thus employing the Italian author's voice as dubbing for their silent series. As subtitles in this book, "Cities & Desire 5" gives the project a substructure of fiction—a literary-architectural addressing of the canal.

The drawing/maps, each paired with a contemporary photograph of the Gowanus Canal area, contrast visionary cartography with the contextual image of our actual city. Simultaneously, Calvino's words serve as fictionalized

2

local history. These aspects of the project as a book—cartographic fiction based on fact, photographs, and narrative fiction—create a duality; the literarily inclined can read *ANGST: Cartography* as an illustrated story, while the architecturally oriented can view it as a sequence of captioned drawings. These elements, encompassing fact and fiction, vision and the visionary, in conjunction with the physical site of the Gowanus Canal, merge to mediate our usual perception of a dilapidated city while simultaneously producing an interpretive guide to one of New York's only functioning canal systems (once popularly known as Lavender Lake, a name stemming from its long—and current—fetid condition).

By examining a disregarded area of New York—one that may soon fade from memory as a toxic inland waterway to become an area prime for development—Baratloo and Balch's *ANGST: Cartography* acknowledges, in advance, an area likely to pass from industrial remnant to historic district, or at least gentrified neighorhood. Their project is introduced by the critic Patricia C. Phillips, who establishes cartographic depiction and map reading as subjective and interpretive activities (akin to fiction/non-fiction) that are also environmentally descriptive. Architectural historian Andrew S. Dolkart contributes the historical bird's-eye perspective for the canal area, demonstrating that history is memory, and providing, for those who wish to read it as such, the antithesis to Calvino's lost history.

ANGST: Cartography is a book of questions, views and thoughts. If the project's voice is tranquil, the vision is piercing, suggesting immediate investigation of the area and evaluation of its significance and social value. Baratloo and Balch have created a beautiful, labyrinthian survey of a quadrant of New York City. They have described and defined the poetics of place:

. . . breeding
Lilacs out of the dead land, mixing
Memory and desire . . .

Patricia C. Phillips

Cartography is the art, or science, of making maps. The map is an iconic representation that leads to illumination, but it is enlightenment that does not necessarily simplify or explain. To illuminate is to depict, and there are many possible depictions (and maps). A consequence of illumination is the revelation that occurs when physical fact and observation intersect with imagination and invention. The map describes a place as well as this process; the cartographer both replicates and conceives.

Recently, I overheard a conversation between two seven-year olds who were examining a globe of the world. As it slowly rotated on its axis, one child traced the equator and described it as an actual line on the earth's surface that attracts the rays of the sun. This unorthodox proposal, delivered with conviction, explained how the sunlight struck the equator and bounced off to heat other, more remote areas of the planet—like New York. From this child's perspective, the fact that the line was depicted meant that it existed to generate a continuous series of magnetic events. The reality of the map-maker's line explained why land masses at zero latitude are warm. Another, more commonly accepted, hypothesis is that the equator is an invented notation to identify locations midway between the poles of rotation, that is the maximum circumference of the globe. The imaginary equatorial line signifies the thickest part of the earth that, because of its dimensionality, is closest to the sun. Heat occurs because of position and propinquity, and not because some line serves as an active allurement. These descriptions, one perhaps more plausible than the other, illuminate ways of thinking about location and phenomena, time and conception, and the often less-than-clear relationship of cause and effect.

ANGST: Cartography is about a constructive resignation to ambiguity and a rejection of polarized thinking. The intellectual convention of the logical in opposition to the illogical is abandoned to embrace the vast variety of depictions that describe events and transformations that influence the substance and perception of place. While there is a withdrawal from the dialectic of the ordered and the arbitrary, there still remains a search for truth. Philosopher Nelson Goodman has examined the flexible relationship of literal and metaphorical truth. They can be the same, or different, but they are both necessary to describe phenomena. Metaphors can be true or false—just like empirically based observations. *ANGST: Cartography* is about this anxious quest for a complicated and rich veracity illuminated through metaphorical and literal images encountered simultaneously.

This is a personal guidebook to a particular place; it is also a general resource that reveals the involute condition of all places. But this guide encourages a different kind of tourist and a more labyrinthian experience of travel. *ANGST: Cartography* wanders its way through an area of Brooklyn that is a fragile, rejected edge in transition; pausing to pick among, and depict, the residue and artifactual record of urban change and vulnerability. It is an aggressive memoir of marginality and an alternative to the typical tourist incentives to "discover" the conspicuous. The inspiring monuments of cities become routinely incised in the collective memory, but it is a passive and directed reminiscence. The encounter with the marginal condition requires tenacious, original, idiosyncratic recollection.

The site of *ANGST: Cartography* is a section along a terminus of the Gowanus Canal. It is a gritty and evolving place. The canal was once a well-traveled thoroughfare for the industries located in the area. Goods were transported on barges along the canal out to New York Bay. The garbage-strewn, malodorous passage is now unused and still for long periods of time. The surrounding blocks accommodate a collection of many abandoned and a few active businesses, including casket-makers, iron-works, oil distributors, and coal storage facilities, some decrepit and some new warehouses, and small residential pockets of frame and brick row houses anchored by corner stores. The precise cut of the canal slices the site with a direct, efficient authority that is in vivid contradistinction to its now decaying and overgrown banks, crumbling piers, and only sporadic use. Although the area is not deserted, there is an overwhelming feeling of abandonment all around. The architectural evidence of a once-thriving area of flourishing enterprises and civic enthusiasms remains, but now there is only the sensation of barren silence (with the exception of a few sounds and signs of renovation and nascent gentrification). Gowanus is one legend of modernity's entropic underside.

This part of Brooklyn is a place that most travelers would not include on their itineraries, and that many of its former inhabitants sought to escape. The decline from industrial vitality to the solemn quiescence of Gowanus is not something that the cartographer normally documents except in the most implicit, unconscious way. Mapping is about the insistence of the present and the erasure of the past. The map is a document of progress, of the establishment of new roads and routes, and the crystallization of new centers and landmarks. *ANGST: Cartography* augments and amends this tradition to include a sensation of time, of ephemera, and of the aspects of place that alter and enrich memory.

Mapping is generally a discursive process, but *ANGST: Cartography* introduces the digressive qualities of speculation. Psychoanalyst Thomas S. Szasz has studied the relationship of epagogic and erratic languages in psychotic and hysterical behaviors.* In discursive language, symbolization is conventional and reasonable. In the non-discursive, it is circuitous and idiosyncratic. The discursive is concrete and presentational. For the psychoanalyst the question is whether the eccentricity of behavior serves an iconic function beyond the spontaneous expression of emotion. How does it communicate a sense of self—or perhaps a sense of place? Does the symptomatic sign have its own syntactical characteristics?

In *ANGST: Cartography*, Moji Baratloo and Clif Balch join both direct and diffusive depictions to suggest a concept of location that conveys the convoluted relationship of the mental and physical landscape and the quiet dread of this discovery. The actual site, its history of development and desolation, and the immediate experience of this decline is explored through a tripartite system of representation. The architects introduce their own process of cartography over an existing map of the site, and, through the use of a grid, divide it into 36 sections. It is an obsessive, maze-like system of markings that records the psychic obstacles of the mind. Each small piece of the site is described by their new map superimposed over an existing map and accompanied by a black and white negative print of a nearby building, space, or detail photographed in situ, as well as a fragment from Italo Calvino's *Invisible Cities* about the furtive, frustrated creation of the city of Zobeide.

Baratloo and Balch's slightly hysterical, idiosyncratic marks seek no particular resolution between the oppressive facts of place and the apocryphal inspiration provided by the Calvino text. Rather, they provide another, iconic system to represent this site and all cities. All places are patterns of private dreams and drawings that never quite congeal into a comprehensible presence. Their map codifies the restless transition and incessant anxiety of place.

ANGST: Cartography confirms the wisdom of the seven-year old who intuitively understood that because the line of the equator has been drawn by the cartographer, a new reality has been inscribed. The map is concurrently a pictograph and an ideograph, an icon and a metaphor. *ANGST: Cartography* is an itinerary that offers no particular route or destination. The phenomenon of place is neither explained nor clarified, but the depiction of its disquietude is passionately rendered.

*Thomas S. Szasz. "Hysteria as Communication," *The Myth of Mental Illness*, Harper & Row, Publishers, Inc. New York, 1961. Reprinted in *Modernism, Criticism, Realism*. Edited by Charles Harrison and Fred Orton. Harper & Row, Publishers. New York. 1984.

ANGST:
Cartography

"Cities & Desire 5" by Italo Calvino

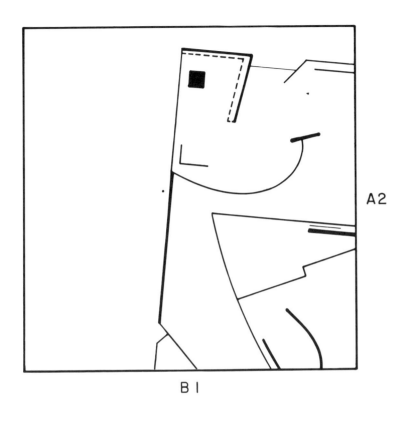

A2

B I

A 1

From there, after six days and seven nights,

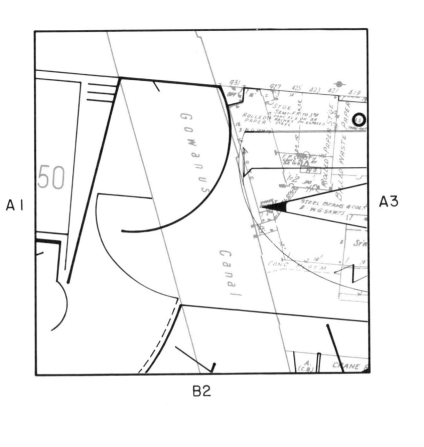

A1   A3

B2

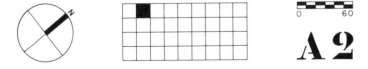

A2

you arrive at Zobeide, the white city, well

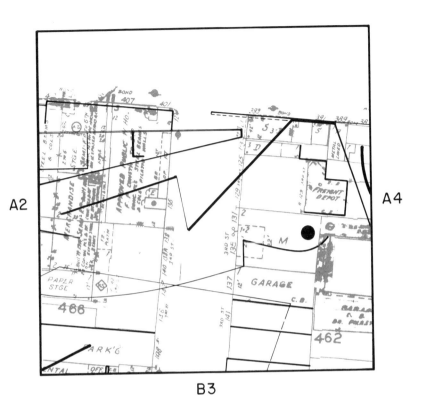

A2   A4

B3

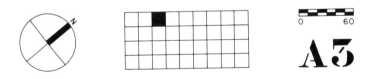

A3

exposed to the moon, with streets wound

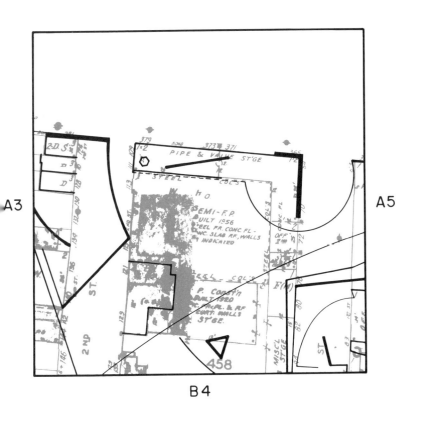

A3

A5

B4

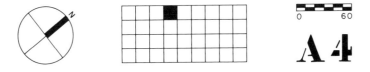

A 4

about themselves as in a skein. They tell this

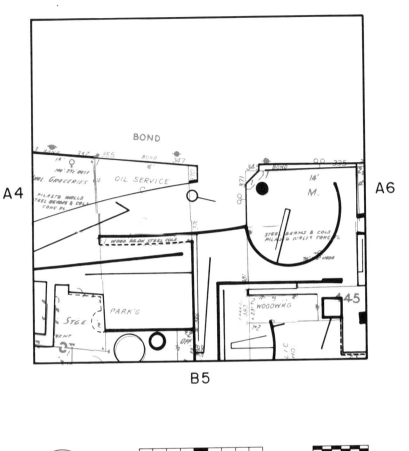

tale of its foundation: men of various nations

THOMAS PAULSON & SON Inc.
CASTINGS
BRONZE
ALUMINUM
BRASS
FOUNDERS
ENGINEERS
450
450

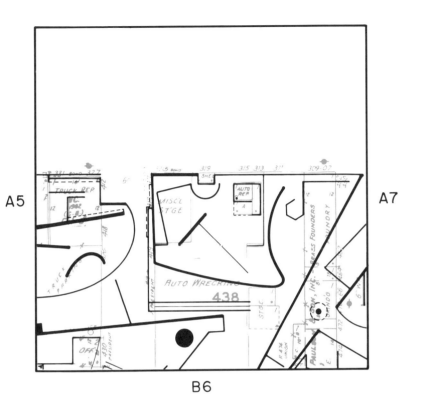

A5

A7

B6

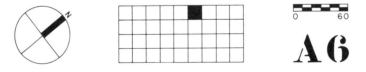

A6

had an identical dream. They saw a woman

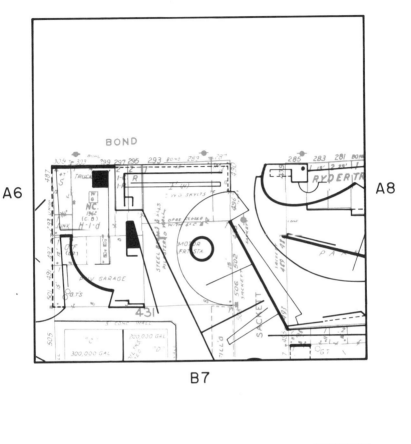

A6

A8

BOND

B7

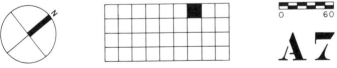

0   60

A 7

running at night through an unknown city; she

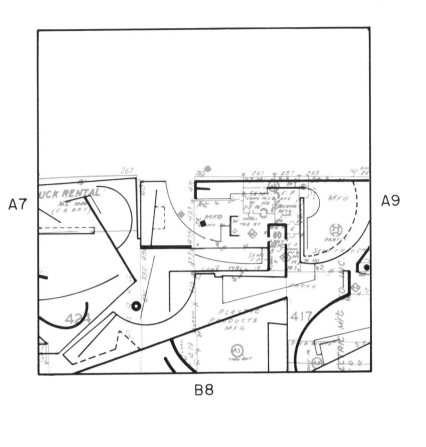

A7

A9

B8

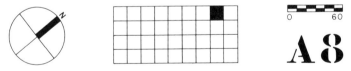

A8

was seen from behind, with long hair, and she

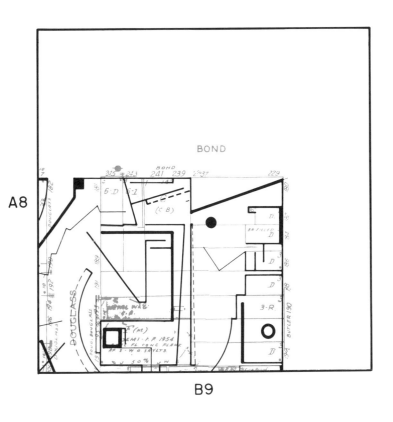

A8

B9

A9

was naked. They dreamed of pursuing her. As

A 1

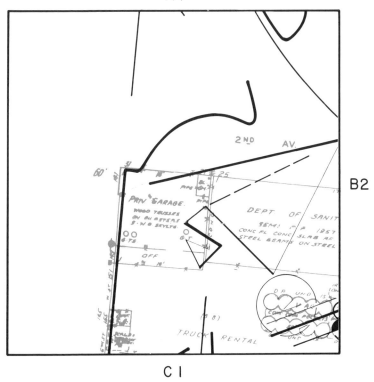

2ND AV.

60'

B2

PRIV GARAGE

WOOD TRUSSES
ON 9" PIERS
9'W 8 SKYLTS

DEPT OF SANIT

SEMI TP 1957
CONC FL CONC SLAB RF
STEEL BEAMS ON STEEL

OFF

TRUCK RENTAL

C 1

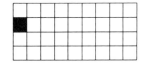

they twisted and turned, each of them lost

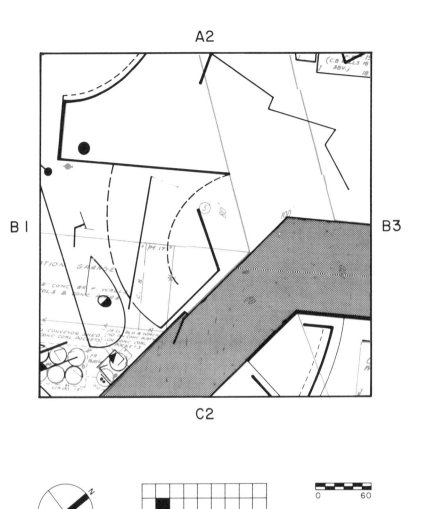

her. After the dream they set out in search of

A3

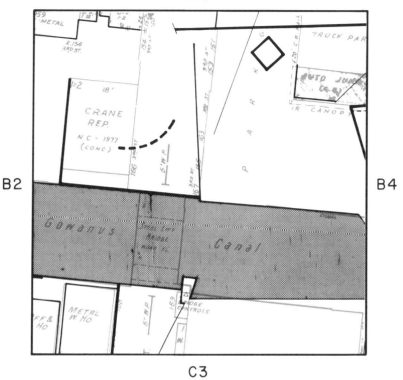

B2

B4

C3

that city; they never found it, but they found

A4

C3

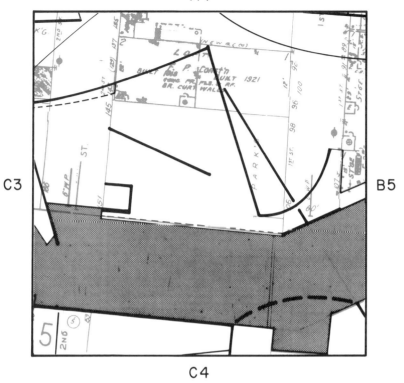

B5

C4

 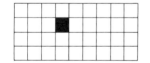

one another; they decided to build a city like

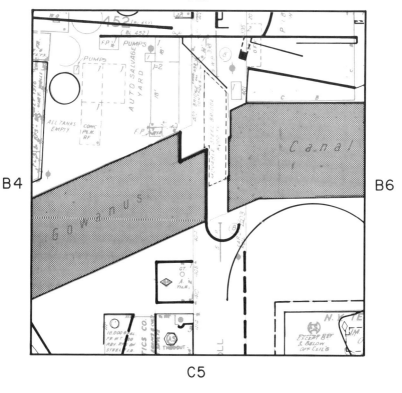

A5

B 4

B 6

C 5

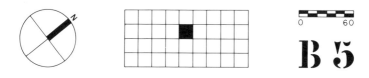

0   60

B 5

the one in the dream. In laying out the streets,

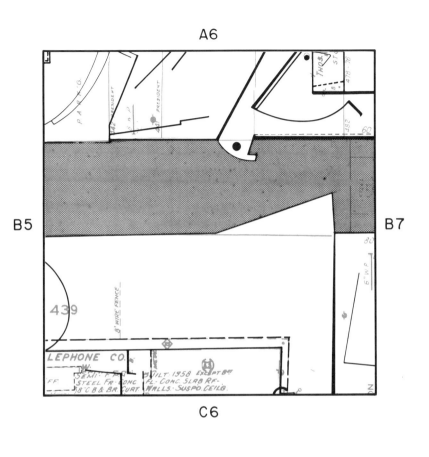

A6

B5   B7

C6

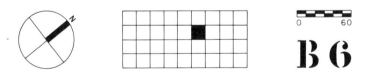

B 6

each followed the course of his pursuit; at the

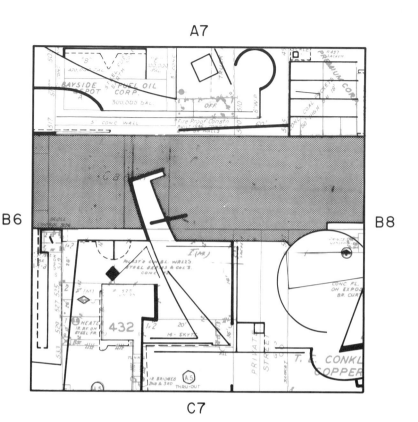

A7

B6

B8

C7

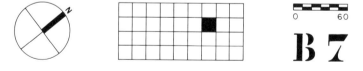

0   60

B 7

spot where they had lost the fugitive's trail,

A8

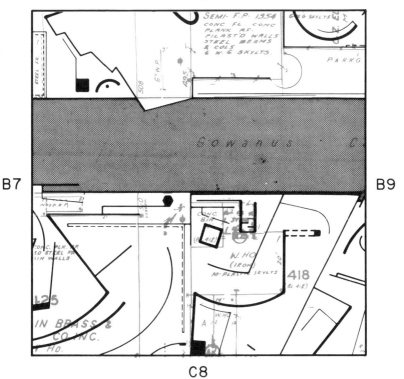

B7

B9

C8

 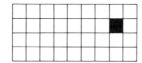

they arranged spaces and walls differently

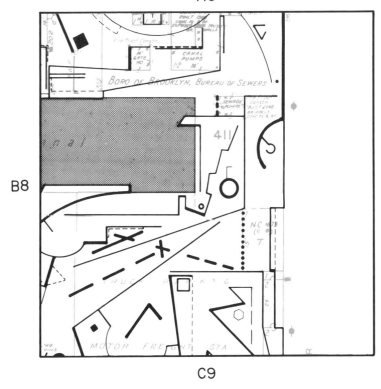

A9

B8

C9

 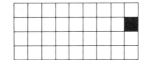

B 9

from the dream, so she would be unable to

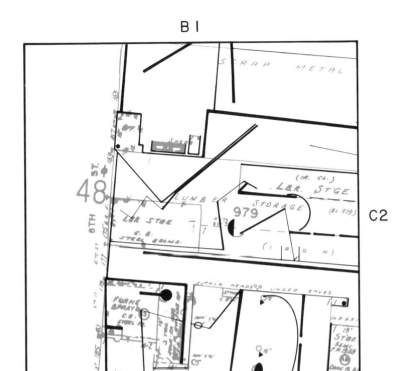

B I

SCRAP METAL

48

6TH ST.

LUMBER

STORAGE

979

(MR. CL.)
L.B.R. STGE

(BL 979)

LBR. STGE
C. B.
STEEL BEAMS.

(I R O N)

C2

SPKLR HEADS UNDER EAVES

FURNC
SPRAY

W. HO.

THRU-OUT

13'
STGE
SEMI.
FIREP.

D I

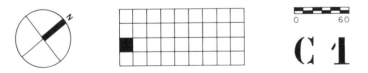

C 1
0   60

escape again. ¶ This was the city of Zobeide,

B2

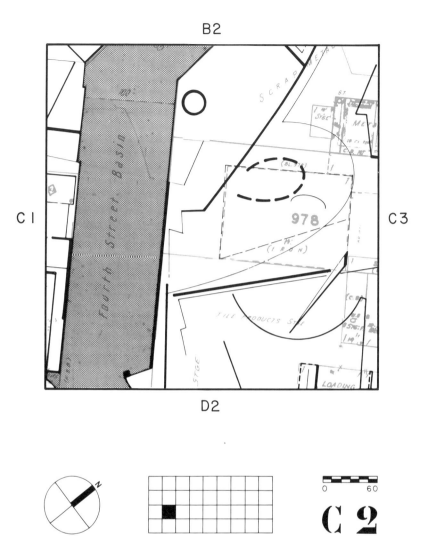

C I

C 3

978

D2

C 2

where they settled, waiting for that scene to

B3

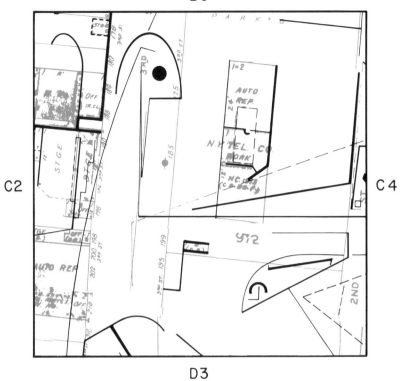

C2

C4

D3

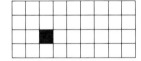

C3

be repeated one night. None of them, asleep

B 4

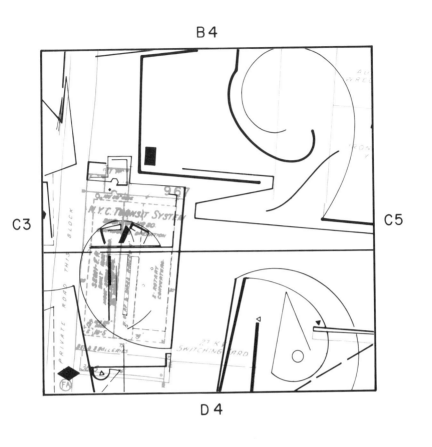

C 3

C 5

D 4

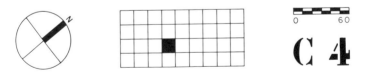

C 4

or awake, ever saw the woman again. The

B5

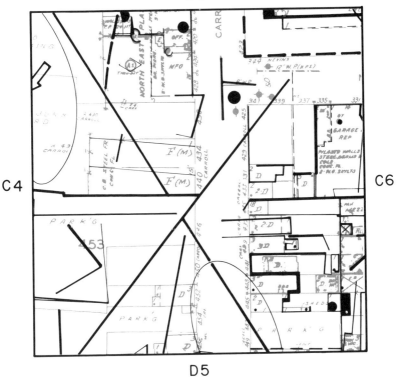

C4

C6

D5

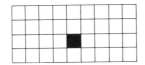

0   60

C 5

city's streets were streets where they went to

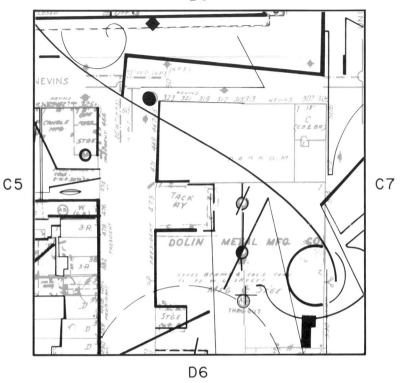

C5 · C7

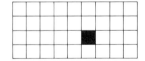

C 6

work every day, with no link any more to the

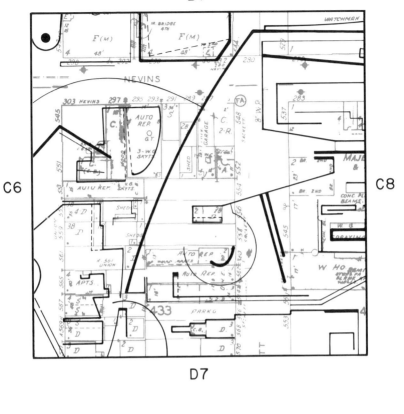

B7

C6

C8

D7

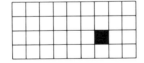

0   60

C 7

dreamed chase. Which, for that matter, had

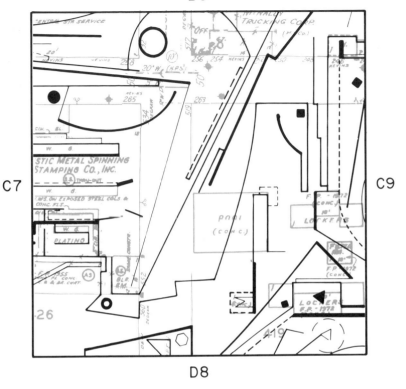

B8

C7

C9

D8

 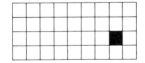

C 8

long been forgotten. ¶ New men arrived from

B9

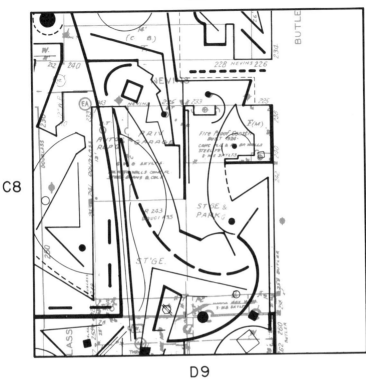

C8

D9

other lands, having had a dream like theirs,

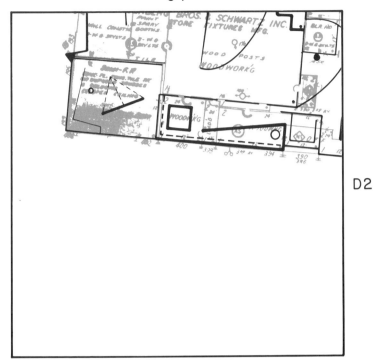

D2

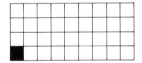

and in the city of Zobeide, they recognized

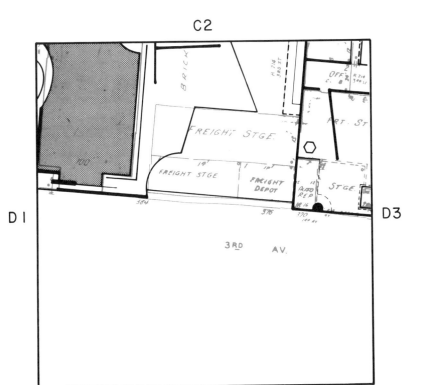

C2

BRICK

H 718
3RD ST

OFF
C.

R 718
340 11

FREIGHT STGE.

PRT. ST

FREIGHT STGE

FREIGHT
DEPOT

AUTO
REP

STGE

100'

D I

D3

504

576

770
100 AV

3 RD   AV.

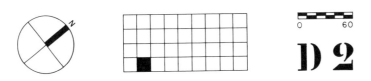

0   60

D 2

something of the streets of the dream, and

C3

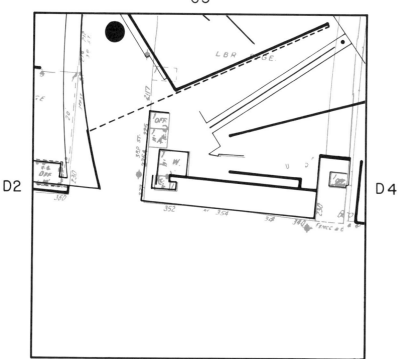

D2

D4

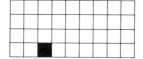

D3

they changed the positions of arcades and

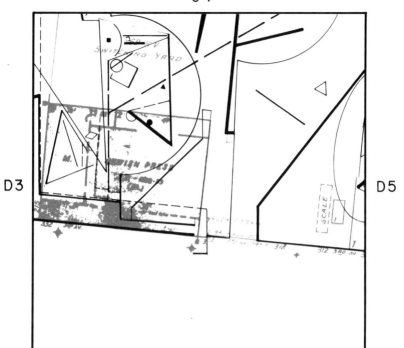

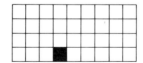

D 4

stairways to resemble more closely the path

C 5

D 4

D 6

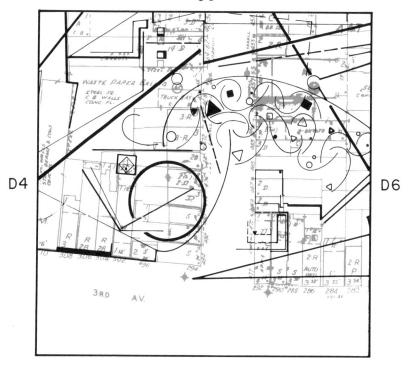

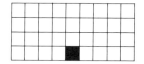

of the pursued woman and so, at the spot

C 6

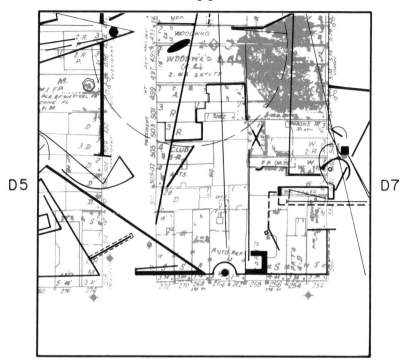

D 5

D 7

 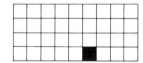

0   60

D 6

where she had vanished, there would remain

SOUTH BROOKLYN
CASKET CO.

534

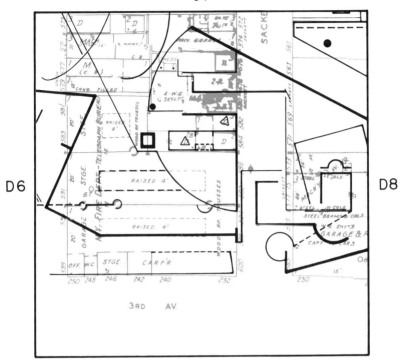

D 7

no avenue of escape. ¶ The first to arrive

C 8

D7

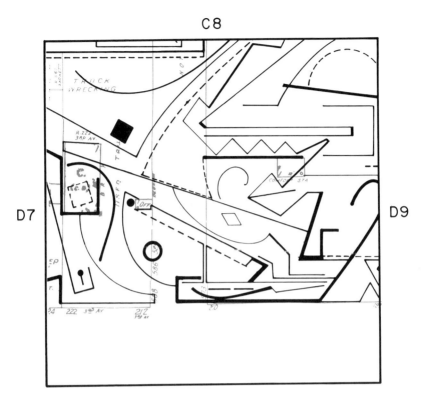

D9

could not understand what drew these people

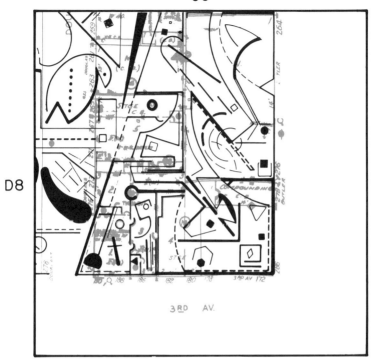

 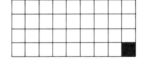

to Zobeide, this ugly city, this trap.

Andrew S. Dolkart

The Gowanus Canal is an anomalous remnant of Brooklyn's industrial past. Best known today for its polluted water and rank odors, the canal retains much of the look of a nineteenth-century commercial waterway, albeit one that has been virtually abandoned by waterborne traffic. Planned as early as the 1840s, but not built until 1867-69, the canal was an extension of Brooklyn's flourishing commercial waterfront. It became the home of a group of prosaic businesses that almost immediately turned the canal into an industrial sewer. The economic viability of the canal declined along with the waterfront in general, and it is now lined primarily with empty lots and abandoned or marginally active factories. Ironically, the fetid canal and its industrial environs are surrounded by increasingly affluent, historic row house neighborhoods, placing the entire area in a transitional state with an unknown future.

The Gowanus Canal lies in the lowlands between the Carroll Gardens and Red Hook sections of the old neighborhood of South Brooklyn to the west and the gentle rise of Park Slope to the east. Prior to the construction of the canal, Gowanus Creek wended its way through the marshy lowlands to Gowanus Bay. During the decades before the canal was built, the elevated areas to the east and west of the creek and marshlands attracted residential development. To the east of the marshes was the early settlement of Gowanus and the Gowanus Road running north/south between present-day Third and Fourth avenues. The community of Gowanus (also spelled Gowanes, Gouwanis, Goujanes, Cojanes and Cujanes) and, by extension, the creek, road, and canal, are said to have been named after Gauwane, an Indian who planted crops in the area. Gowanus has been traced to the word "cowanes," meaning briar. The settlement of Gowanus is still evident today in the area around 12th Street and Fourth Avenue where a large number of early, peak-roofed wooden houses survive.

Gowanus Creek and its adjoining marshlands remained largely undeveloped until after the Civil War. According to a 1916 publication celebrating the 75th anniversary of *The Brooklyn Daily Eagle*, "Gowanus Bay in 1867 still breathed the atmosphere of a rustic past, and was the anchorage of nothing but pleasure boats." Although this description is somewhat romanticized (construction of piers and warehouses had already begun along the north shore of the bay), it does indicate the relative tranquility of the area, a tranquility that was rapidly destroyed by Brooklyn's expanding commercial facilities and by the related construction of the Gowanus Canal.

Brooklyn is rarely thought of today as a great industrial and commercial power, but during the latter half of the nineteenth century,

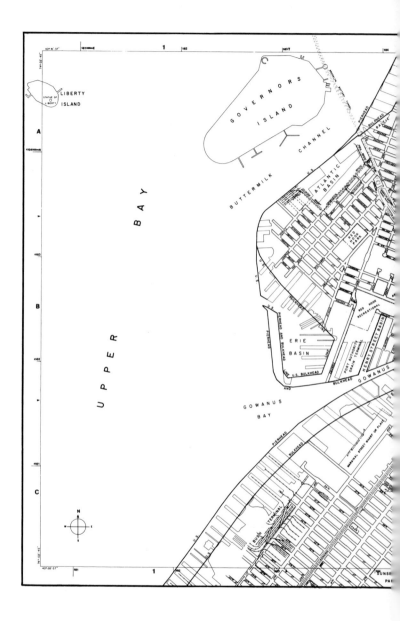

New York City, Section 16—Borough of Brooklyn

FORT
GREENE
PARK

P R O S P E C T   P A R K

BROOKLYN BOTANIC GARDEN

ZOOLOGICAL GARDENS

PROSPECT
LAKE

PARADE GROUNDS

REENWOOD

C E M E T E R Y

New York City Department of City Planning

91

the independent city of Brooklyn developed into one of the major industrial and warehousing centers in America. Much of this development occurred along the waterfront, especially in the area between Greenpoint and Red Hook. In the 1840s, the Brooklyn waterfront started to become a regional center for the handling of bulk cargoes. Beginning with the creation of the Atlantic Basin (1841-47) along the western shore of Red Hook, docks, basins, and warehouses for the storage and shipment of grain, tobacco, coffee, and other produce were constructed. These warehouse facilities flourished because of the tremendous activity generated by the Erie Canal. So many warehouses were erected along the shoreline that Brooklyn was nicknamed "the walled city."

In 1856, construction began on a second major shipping basin, located south of the Atlantic Basin at the southern end of Red Hook. This was the Erie Basin. With its breakwater and long piers (including the spectacular warehouse pier at the end of Van Brunt Street), the Erie Basin became one of the major grain storage facilities in the port. Created primarily out of drained and dredged wetlands and swamps, the Erie Basin formed a narrow entrance into Gowanus Bay and, after its construction in the late 1860s, into the Gowanus Canal.

Two notable structures relating to the grain trade survive near the entrance to the canal. The most prominent of these is the concrete grain elevator erected in 1920-22 on Gowanus Bay, just cast of the Erie Basin at the terminal of the New York Barge Canal. Unique in New York City, this elevator has a capacity of 2,000,000 bushels of grain. Never a successful financial venture, the elevator has been closed since 1965. Farther north, at the entrance to the canal, is one of the most beautiful of Brooklyn's grain warehouses, the former Bowne Stores, facing the canal at Creamer and Smith streets. Built c.1880, this is a boldly massed, four-story brick structure with original cast-iron shutters.

As the vast warehouse complexes rose along the shoreline, more marginal businesses, such as coal yards, lumber yards, and gas works, which needed large waterfront sites, found it increasingly difficult to find appropriate land. Such firms moved to the new Gowanus Canal. The idea for creating a canal along the route of Gowanus Creek was first suggested in the 1840s. In 1847, Brooklyn businessman and developer Daniel Richards petitioned the Brooklyn Common Council for permission to open streets in South Brooklyn, not far from the Atlantic and Erie basins, both of which Richards had helped to initiate. At the same time, Richards proposed the construction of a barge canal along Gowanus Creek. It was not, however, until 1867 that the New York State Legislature passed a bill providing for the dredging of the creek and the construction of docks. One year later, the Legislature established the Gowanus Canal Improvement Commission, which was empowered to construct a canal between Douglass and Percival streets. Work immediately began on the main canal and, shortly thereafter, on five basins (four survive) that extend the canal into the drained marshlands to the east.

As soon as it was completed, businesses that relied on water transport for the delivery and transshipment of goods opened along the canal. An 1869 atlas of Brooklyn shows that several lumber yards, a lime factory, and a cement works had already located there. Although there was still some vacant land along the canal in the 1880s, Henry Stiles was able to report in his 1886 publication, *Civil, Political, Professional, and Ecclesiastical History of Kings County and the City of Brooklyn,* that "immense lumber yards, coal yards, and flouring and plaster and other mills, and brick and stone yards, occupy the whole available space."

Besides the many mills, coal and lumber yards, the canal attracted a large number of noxious industries that used the canal to dump their wastes. Among these were gas, creosote, tartar, ammonia, glass, oil, chemical, and lime works. Many of these businesses did not need large permanent buildings, but relied on wooden structures and open lots. Only a few erected large masonry factories or warehouses, several of which are still standing. The most prominent of these is the late Romanesque Revival style former power plant standing to the east of the canal at 2nd Street. Erected in 1902 by the Brooklyn Rapid Transit Railroad and later used by the New York City Transit Authority, this massive abandoned brick building looms over its surroudings.

Also of interest are the imposing buildings of the Empire City Hygeia Ice Company on Bond Street. The complex was later used as a paper warehouse and the canal facade still retains a faded painted sign advertising the company.

Complaints about the unhealthy quality of the Gowanus Canal began to be heard soon after its completion. By 1888, conditions had become so unsalutary that a medical committee was appointed to study the effects of the canal. In a series of articles printed in September 1888, *The World* reported on the committee's progress, observing that "they are marching slowly along the murky banks of the canal; taking in its smells and discovering something new and surprising in that line every day." *The World* condemned the canal, calling it a "cesspool" and a "blot on American civilization," and quoted a doctor as saying that it was breeding malaria, typhoid, scarlet fever, and diphtheria. The 1888 investigation had no impact, and the canal was to remain one of the most blighted areas of Brooklyn. Throughout the twentieth century, efforts were made to clean up what had come to be known as "Lavender Lake." In 1906, a sewage treatment plant was built at the northern end of the canal, but the waters remained as polluted as ever.

The Gowanus Canal is a tidal waterway one hundred feet wide and originally twelve to sixteen feet deep at high water (the present depth is somewhat lower). The main part of the canal stretches southward from midway between Butler and Douglass streets to Hamilton Street, where it widens as it meets Gowanus Bay. The canal was constructed with wooden bulkheads, many of which are extant and contribute to the waterway's timeworn quality.

The canal is crossed by five street-level bridges that are opened for the occasional barge still traversing the waterway. One of these, the Carroll Street Bridge, is the only officially designated landmark in the area. Built in 1888-89, the Carroll Street Bridge is one of the oldest bridges in New York City, and the oldest of four known "retractile" bridges in America. The steel bridge, built by Cooper, Hewitt & Co., rests on rollers and, when in operation, retracts diagonally across the channel to an adjacent piece of land. The bridge is now in a permanently open position awaiting extensive rehabilitation. Among the most visible features of the Gowanus Canal area are two structures that soar above the canal: the Gowanus Expressway crosses the canal on a modern steel viaduct erected in the 1950s, and the IND's F train rattles by on a dramatic concrete viaduct completed in 1933.

By the mid-twentieth century, activity on the Gowanus Canal had ebbed, reflecting the general decline of the entire Brooklyn waterfront. With improved land transport, most businesses located along the canal no longer needed to rely on water for their shipping. Many of the companies abandoned their factories and moved out of New York City; other buildings were converted for marginal uses or were demolished. Although the canal area has stagnated, it probably does not look too different today than it did in its heyday. The combination of a polluted waterway lined with brick factories (some old and some new) and open lots used for the storage of lumber, building materials, heating oil and other products, conforms with the canal area's original industrial use.

LIST OF PHOTOGRAPHS

99

B3 - Steel Lift Bridge, Third Street.

B4 - *Chem Trader*, Foot of Second Street.

B5 - Control House, Carroll Street Bridge.

B6 - Operating Schedule, Union Street Bridge.

B7 - Coal Pockets, Sackett Street.

B8 - Concrete Coal Bin, DeGraw Street.

B9 - Wooden Bulkheads, North End of Canal.

C1 - Furniture Factory, Sixth Street.

C2 - Lumber Shed, Fourth Street Basin.

C3 - Pallet Yard Gate, Third Street.

C4 - Sub-Station No. 20, Second Street.

C5 - Plastics Factory, Carroll Street.

C6 - Security Barrier, President Street.

C7 - Driveway with Bridge, Nevins Street.

C8 - Metal Chimney, DeGraw Street.

C9 - Water Supply Station, Butler Street.

D1 - Boiler House, Third Avenue.

D2 - Coal Pockets, Fourth Street Basin.

D3 - Gas Station, Third Avenue.

D4 - Truck Scale, Third Avenue.

D5 - Parking Lot, Carroll Street.

D6 - Fire Escape, President Street.

D7 - Casket Company, Union Street.

D8 - Basketball Court, Double ''D'' Playground.

D9 - Oil Tanks, Butler Street.

NOTES AND ACKNOWLEDGMENTS

Originally drawn at a scale of 1″ = 60', the 36 cartographic plates and the fold-out map of *ANGST:
Cartography* have been reduced for publication
to 1″ = 100' and 1″ = 200' respectively.

The 36 photographs, taken from spring to
autumn of 1988, each correspond to the actual
area defined by the cartographic plate on the facing page. Some of the artifacts pictured, such as
(B5) Control House, Carroll Street Bridge, no
longer exist.

Six years have passed since our first visit to

the industrial ruins of the Gowanus Canal in 1982. During this time we have been fortunate in receiving generous encouragement and assistance throughout the various manifestations of *ANGST: Cartography*.

Frank Shifreen first introduced us to the Gowanus Canal through *The Monument Redefined* exhibition.

Kyong Park and the Storefront for Art & Architecture exhibited the original drawing, and have maintained an invaluable creative forum.

Glenn Weiss provided timely criticism and the opportunity to exhibit *ANGST: Cartography* at The Institute for Contemporary Art, P.S. 1 Museum.

Joshua Decter and The Institute for Contemporary Art encouraged and facilitated the installation concept at P.S. 1 Museum.

Plauto, with craft and patience, helped us to realize the photographic images.